TREVOR
AND THE HUNT
GOLDEN

For Lily and Evie

Published 2020 by Keith Putman. Text and Illustrations copyright Keith Putman 2020
The right of Keith Putman to be identified as the Author and Illustrator of this work has
been asserted by him in accordance with the Copyright, Designs and Patents Act 1988.
ISBN 9780995490826

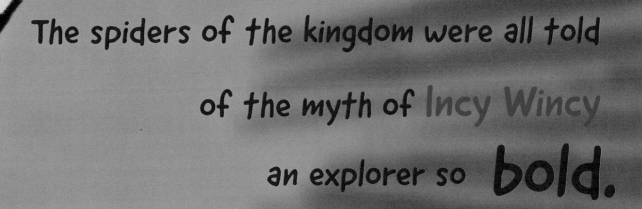

The spiders of the kingdom were all told

of the myth of Incy Wincy

an explorer so **bold.**

Though some called him a hero
a brave adventurer and a Star.

Some called him a crazy dreamer
for exploring so far.

Incy spent his time searching
for a prize so rare.
Which he believed was hidden
in the fly kings lair.

He packed and waved goodbye

to start his hunt for the elusive . . .

GOLDEN
FLY

Incy's grandson is called Trevor.
Although he is only young,
he is brave, curious and clever.

He dreamed of following his Grandad and becoming an explorer as well. "Only when you're grown up" his mother would yell.

Ten years had past
and Trevor was grown up at last.
He trained night and day
to improve his swinging, map reading
and learn the explorers way.

One day while out exploring
Trevor discovered a chest hidden
under the flooring.

The chest was left behind

by grandad Incy Wincy,

What a find!

Trevor's mission was clear:
- follow the map he found
- make his Grandad proud
- discover the fly so renowned

Trevor put on his new hat and rucksack.
He then said goodbye to all his family.
He had no idea when he'd be back.

First he had to find a way across
the land of giants and dangers unknown.
He spun his line and prepared his swing.
His first step towards the fly kings throne.

Secretly Trevor must sneakily sneak past a huge furry menace that moves so fast.

Trevor swung a mighty swing knowing that

one false move and he'd go **SPLAT**

Boingy Boingy Boingy Boing

off Trevor flew.

Trevor swung even though he was scared.

The red tongue shot out but Trevor was prepared.

Trevor
landed safe
and sound.
What
amazing
luck!

The sticky web struck
and the beasts tongue
was stuck.

The tunnel
was dark and damp,
but look...

...was that his Grandad's camp?

Trevor could see the entrance
to the famous drain.
He was so close but down came the

Rain Rain Rain.

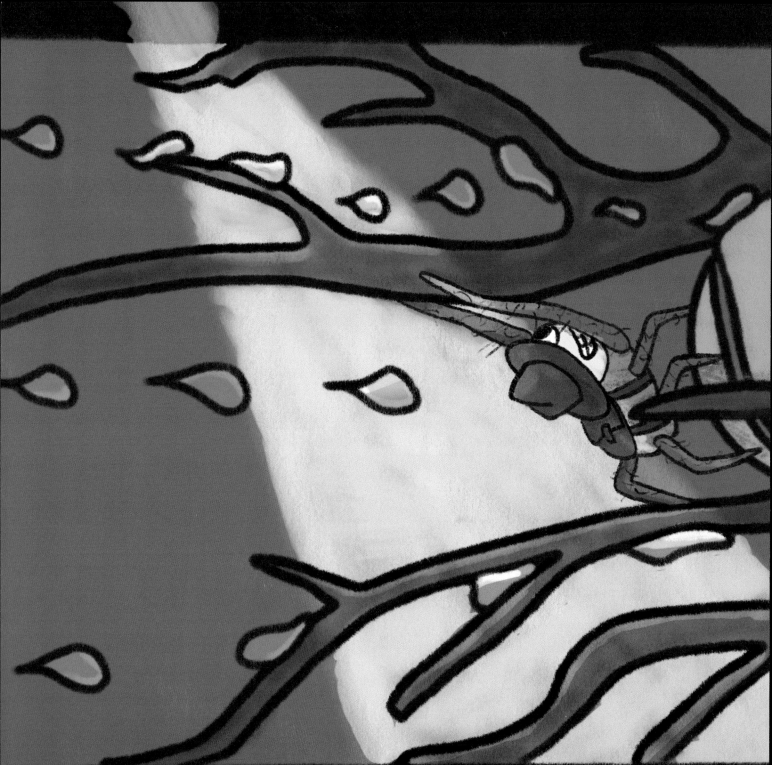

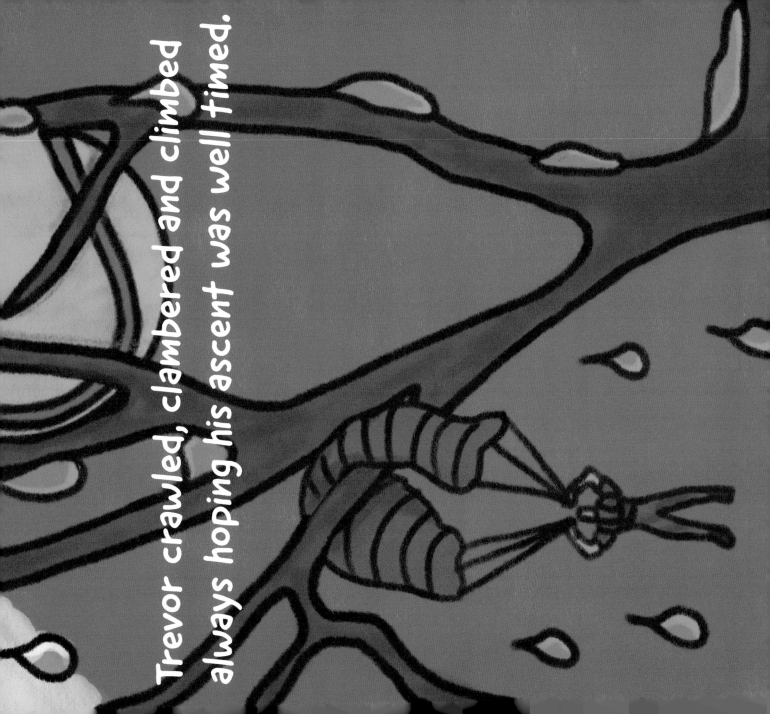

Trevor crawled, clambered and climbed always hoping his ascent was well timed.

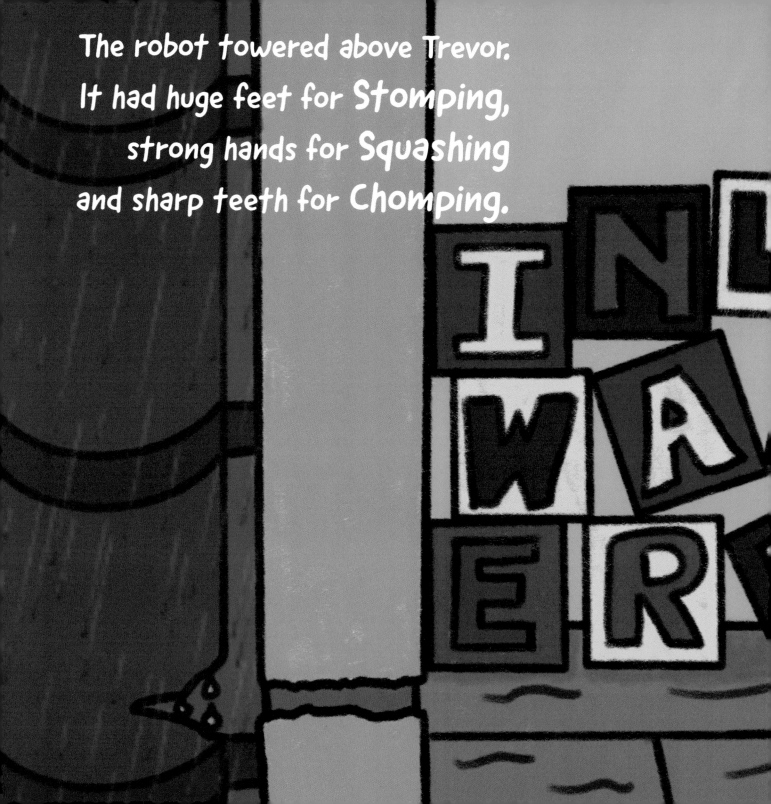

The robot towered above Trevor.
It had huge feet for Stomping,
strong hands for Squashing
and sharp teeth for Chomping.

Trevor looked up.
He was very fearful
but the giants face
he realised was ...

" Hello there little spider" said Ronnie
the robot in a deep vibrating voice.
"I hope I didn't scare you with my big head.
Would you like to be friends? Your choice."

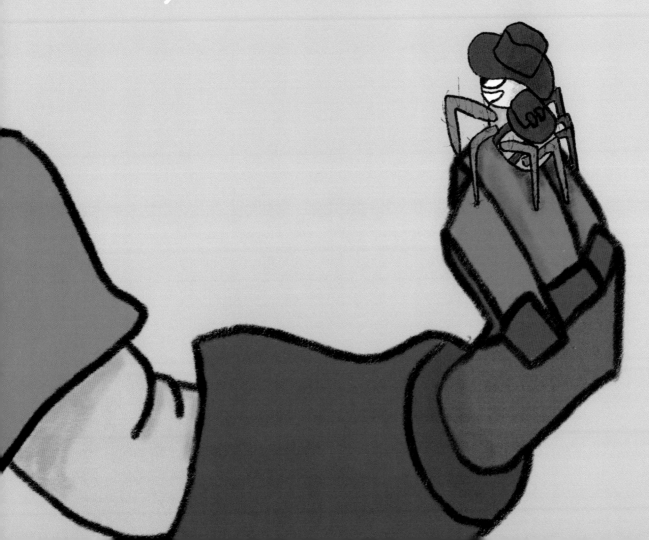

The robot had helped Incy years before
and aided him on his mission to explore.

Ronnie says "I know where the fly castle lies,"
he then raised Trevor towards the skies.

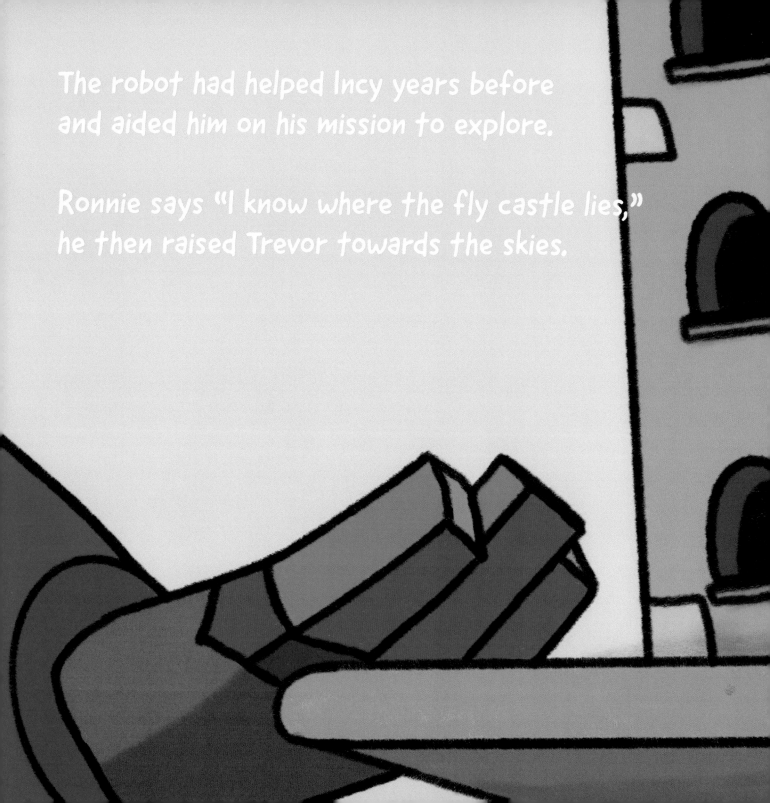

The fly castle loomed up ahead.
Trevor pushed on through the gate
even though he was filled with dread.

At last the treasure room was insight
but its entrance was barred.
Two armoured fly soldiers stood alert,
how would Trevor outwit the guard?

A plan was formed
and Trevor begun
to lay his trap.

Lured in by
a whistle
the fly's wings
began to flap.

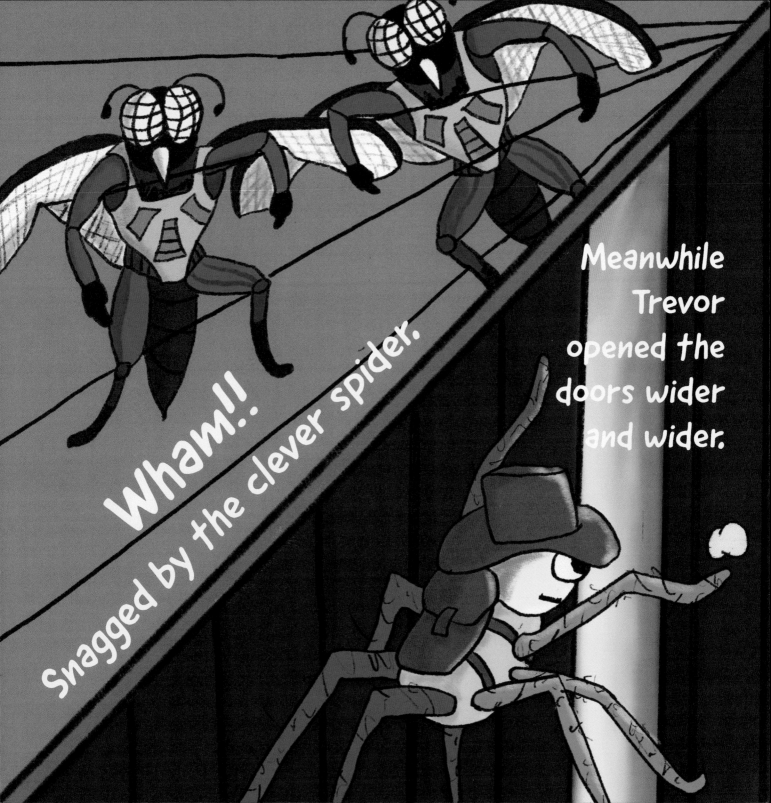

Before his eyes lay a treasure, an end to a quest and a wealth beyond measure.

But if the golden fly remained
and his Grandad had failed his goal.
Whatever happened to Incy Wincy?
Wait ... is that a scroll?

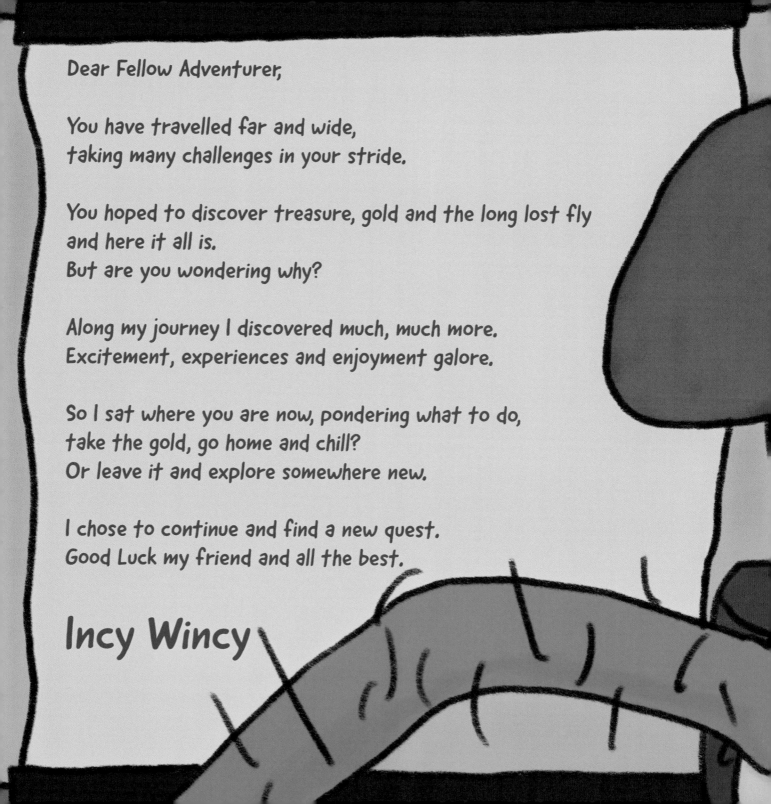

Dear Fellow Adventurer,

You have travelled far and wide,
taking many challenges in your stride.

You hoped to discover treasure, gold and the long lost fly
and here it all is.
But are you wondering why?

Along my journey I discovered much, much more.
Excitement, experiences and enjoyment galore.

So I sat where you are now, pondering what to do,
take the gold, go home and chill?
Or leave it and explore somewhere new.

I chose to continue and find a new quest.
Good Luck my friend and all the best.

Incy Wincy

Printed in Poland
by Amazon Fulfillment
Poland Sp. z o.o., Wrocław

64448391R00026